Dick and Jane

READING COLLECTION • VOLUME 10

W9-BQL-884

We Work

GROSSET & DUNLAP • NEW YORK

Work

Work, Dick.
Work, work.

See, see.

See Dick work.

Oh, Dick.

See, see.

Oh, oh, oh.

See Sally Work

Work, work, work.

Sally can work.

See Sally work

Oh, Dick.

Oh, Jane.

See, see.

Sally can work.

Oh, Sally.

Funny, funny Sally.

Oh, oh, oh.

Funny Sally

See Father work.

Work, work, work.

Father can work.

See Sally work.

Work, work, work.

Sally can work.

Oh, Father.

See, see.

Sally can work.

Oh, Sally.
Funny, funny Sally.

Who Can Help?

See Jane.

Jane can work.

Jane can help.

Jane can help Mother.

Jane can help Mother work.

Father can help Jane.

See It Work

Father said, "Look, Sally.
See something big.
You can see it work.
Up, up it comes.
See it work."

Sally said, "See it work.
Work, work, work."

"Help, help," said Sally.
"See my little Tim go down.
Jump down, Father.
I want my little Tim."

"Oh, Sally," said Father.
"I can not jump down.
I can not help you."

"Oh, see it work," said Dick.
"See it come up, up, up.
Up comes Tim to Baby
Sally."

"Up, up," said Sally.
"Up comes my little Tim.
Up comes Tim to Sally."

We Make Something

"Look here," said Dick.

"I can make something funny.

I can make Spot.

Spot is red and blue."

"Oh, Dick," said Jane.

"I want to make something.

I want to make something blue."

"Look, Sally," said Jane.
"See my funny blue Puff.
Make something, Sally.
Make something blue."

"Oh, Jane," said Sally.
"I can not make Puff.
I can not make Spot.
I want to make little Tim."

"See me work," said Sally.
"I can make something blue.
See my funny blue Tim."

"Look, Sally," said Jane.
"Here is something for Tim.
Here is a funny red mother.
And a funny blue father.
A father and mother for Tim."

Spot Finds Something

Dick said, "Come and work.
Come and help me.
I can not find the two boats.
I can not find my red ball.
Where is my yellow boat?
Where is the blue boat?
Where is my little red ball?
Where, oh, where?"

Jane said, "I can work.

I can find two boats.

Here is the yellow boat.

Here is the blue boat."

Sally said, "I can find cars.

See my little yellow car.

See my red car and my blue car.

Where is the red ball?

Where is my little Tim?"